W9-CRO-137

MAKE YOUR OWN ADVENTURE

WOOLLYFOOT'S BIG RACE

Illustrations by Colin Petty
Written by Stewart Cowley

DERRYDALE BOOKS
NEW YORK

Published 1985 by
Derrydale Books
Distributed by
Crown Publishers, Inc.

Produced for Derrydale Books by
Victoria House Publishing Ltd.,
4/5 Lower Borough Walls,
Bath BA1 1QR, England.

Copyright © 1985 Victoria House
Publishing Ltd.

All rights reserved. No part of this
publication may be reproduced, stored
in a retrieval system, or transmitted, in
any form or by any means, electronic,
mechanical, photocopying, recording
or otherwise without the prior
permission of the copyright holder.

Printed in Belgium.

THE ADVENTURE

A little bragging in a neighboring village lands champion runner Woollyfoot in the race of his lifetime. While his rival speeds along twisting mountain roads, Woollyfoot's path takes him across country toward unknown adventures.

Will Woollyfoot win? As you read the story, you will discover that there are decisions to be made — look for the signposts on the pages. Often there will be two choices with a different page number beside each one. When you have decided what Woollyfoot should do, turn to the page number shown, and discover where you have led him! If you're not given a choice, the signposts will show you the way.

Have a good adventure, and remember, the choice is yours!

Woollyfoot was the champion runner of Meadowfree. When he went to visit his friends in Glitterbrook, he never expected that adventures awaited him.

Glitterbrook was famous for the speed of its cyclists and, as usual, Woollyfoot soon got into an argument about who was the fastest.

"I could bike to Meadowfree before you were even halfway there!" declared Rumblewheel.

"Nonsense!" laughed Woollyfoot. "Even if I ran I would win."

"Let's have a race!" cried the Mayor. "Maybe that will stop your bragging!"

Woollyfoot and Rumblewheel started off as everyone cheered. The villagers were to travel to Meadowfree later by riverboat.

Rumblewheel pedaled furiously down the road and Woollyfoot waved cheerily as he raced up the hillside.

But soon after, Woollyfoot ran into a thick fog. He peered hopelessly into the gloom. "I'm lost!" he thought. "Should I keep going on or wait for the fog to clear?"

KEEP GOING   12

WAIT   8

Hours later, the fog finally lifted and Woollyfoot found he was near a little cottage. It sat at the edge of a big forest. He started to run toward the house. Maybe there might be someone there who could help him find the fastest way to Meadowfree.

He was dodging through the bushes near the forest when he heard the sound of singing. Peeping through a bush, he saw a group of tiny people scooping up mud from the banks of a stream. More

8

little folk were loading it onto small, brightly painted wagons.

A delicious smell of cooking drifted down from the cottage. "Mmm, I'm hungry!" thought Woollyfoot. "Those little people might know the best way to Meadowfree—but I would like something to eat."

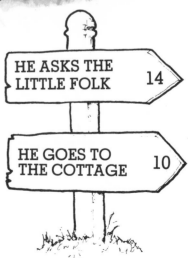

HE ASKS THE LITTLE FOLK   14

HE GOES TO THE COTTAGE   10

9

"Rap, tap!" Woollyfoot knocked on the door. It swung open, and standing before him was a cheery old man. Woollyfoot told him he had been lost in the fog. "And," he finished, "I'm starving!"

"Well," said the Woodman, for that's who he was, "I'm just cooking some dinner. Come in." Woollyfoot ate three big platefuls before he remembered why he had knocked.

"Can you," he asked between mouthfuls, "tell me the way to Meadowfree?"

"I only know this part of the forest," replied the Woodman, "but there is a signpost nearby." He cleared up the dishes and asked Woollyfoot—who after all had eaten a very great deal—if he would help gather wood for the kilns of the Pixie Potters.

"They must be the little people who were singing," thought Woollyfoot. "The Woodman has been very kind, but I really should find out what the signpost says."

HE HELPS THE WOODMAN 16

HE GOES TO THE SIGNPOST 18

11

Woollyfoot stumbled through the fog for hours. As it began to clear he came across a wide, cobbled road. In the middle stood two red-faced people who were shouting at each other. They stopped when they saw Woollyfoot.

"Who are you?" asked Woollyfoot.

"I'm Bicker and he's Quibble," said one.

"It's the other way around!" cried the other angrily.

"Oh no it's not," was the reply.

"Never mind," interrupted Woollyfoot. "Do you always argue about everything?"

"No!" said one.

"Yes!" said the other.

"I just want to know the quickest way to Meadowfree," sighed Woollyfoot.

"It's up the hill past Cloudbanger's castle," replied one.

"No, it's down the road and over the bridge," shouted the other—and they both stamped off. Woollyfoot listened to them quarreling until they were out of sight.

"Well, it must be one way or the other," he thought.

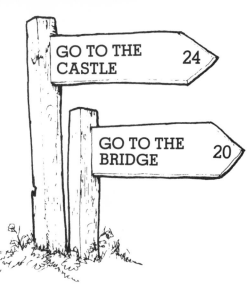

GO TO THE CASTLE   24

GO TO THE BRIDGE   20

Woollyfoot stepped out from behind the bush and walked up to the closest of the happy group. A little fellow looked up.

"Oh!" he gasped. "You frightened me." The others gathered around. They told him they were the Pixie Potters. "Have you come to help us dig clay for our pots?" asked one.

"Well, no," answered Woollyfoot, and he told them about the race. "So you see," said Woollyfoot, "I'm trying to get to Meadowfree."

"Hmm, there is a road, but the old bridge you have to cross is

not very safe. We never use it," said one pixie, thoughtfully. "But if you help us fill the wagons you can come to our camp. Our chief might know another way."

Woollyfoot knew that the bridge might be dangerous, but the wagons were only half full—he might lose time if he stayed with the pixies.

HE HELPS 16

HE GOES TO THE BRIDGE 20

15

When the work was done, Woollyfoot went to the pixie camp. There he helped the pixies fill the kilns with wood.

The chief was very grateful. "This stream leads to the river that runs through Meadowfree," he told Woollyfoot. "You could use one of our pottery boats. It would be swift but I don't know how safe it would be. The current is quite strong."

"Isn't there any other way?" Woollyfoot asked nervously.

The pixie chief thought for a moment. "You could ask the Riddler. He knows all the paths, but you can never get a straight answer from him. You'll find him at the crossroads."

HE ASKS THE RIDDLER   18

HE TAKES THE BOAT   28

THE LONG WAY H

Woollyfoot ran and ran until he came to an old, ivy-covered sign-post. A strange, tattered figure stood there.

"Who are you?" Woollyfoot asked.

"I'm the Riddler," replied the ragged man. "Ask me something."

Woollyfoot looked up at the sign that said The Long Way Home and The Short Way Home. "Which is the quickest way?" he asked.

"Aha," smiled the Riddler. "Listen to my rhyme. Then you can decide." And he began to sing . . . .

18

THE SHORT WAY HOME

The short way is the hard way
But the shortest way, although
The long way is the easy way
But a longer way, you know.
The hardness of the short way
Can make it very slow.
The long way though it's easier,
Is a longer way to go.

GO THE LONG WAY 24

GO THE SHORT WAY 22

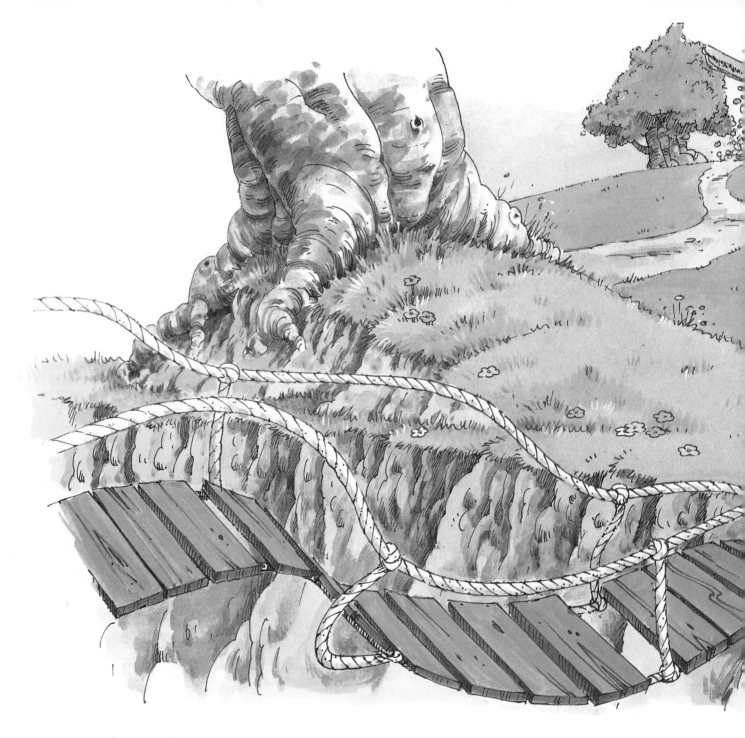

At last Woollyfoot could see the bridge. Suddenly, in a cloud of dust, Rumblewheel hurtled down the road, rattled across the bridge and disappeared around a corner.

"This *must* be the right road," cried Woollyfoot, and he raced up to the rickety bridge. It creaked and swayed as he ran across and then, with a loud groan, it began to collapse. With a mighty leap Woollyfoot reached the other side—just as the bridge crashed into

the river far below! He sat down on a grassy hill to catch his breath.

A track led up the steep hillside and Woollyfoot could see a signpost outlined against the sky. "That might show me a quick way home," he thought. "Or I could follow Rumblewheel along the road . . ."

HE FOLLOWS RUMBLEWHEEL 22

HE CLIMBS THE HILL 18

21

Running like the wind, Woollyfoot felt sure he was catching up to Rumblewheel but suddenly he skidded to a halt. Huge boulders and clumps of mud had spilled down the cliff and blocked the path.

"Oh no!" gasped Woollyfoot. The road zig-zagged down the mountain. At the bottom it curved along a large lake.

"There's Rumblewheel!" he cried. Sure enough, the Glitterbrook cyclist was racing along the road ahead of him. Desperately, Woollyfoot looked around. An old stepped path led precariously down the mountain.

"I could climb down there," he muttered to himself. "Or I could dive into the lake—it looks deep enough."

| HE DIVES | 38 |

| HE CLIMBS DOWN | 32 |

23

Woollyfoot had walked for what seemed like hours when he came to a huge castle. A fast flowing river ran under the drawbridge and a small boat floated close by.

There was no sign of life from the castle and Woollyfoot wondered if there was anyone inside who could show him how to get to Meadowfree.

"The gate seems to be open so I suppose I could go in and see," he thought. "But if this river is running in the right direction it would be much quicker. I could always return the boat later and thank the owner."

HE TAKES
THE BOAT   28 ➤

HE ENTERS
THE CASTLE 26 ➤

25

Woollyfoot stepped into a dim hallway.

"Hello," he called. "Is anyone home?" A flight of stairs spiraled upward and he climbed higher and higher until he came to a huge door. It was open so he tiptoed in. A gust of wind slammed the door behind him. Woollyfoot tried to reach the handle, but it was too high up. He was trapped in Cloudbanger's bedroom—

26

and Cloudbanger was a giant!

"Oh no!" gasped Woollyfoot. "He's sure to be cross if I wake him. He's so big!"

He looked out of a window and saw that he was in a high tower. "I know," he thought, spotting a pile of sheets. "I can make a rope from these. Or maybe even a parachute!"

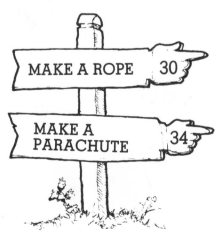

MAKE A ROPE 30

MAKE A PARACHUTE 34

27

Woollyfoot climbed into the boat and cast off. The current gripped the boat and swept it along faster and faster. Somewhere ahead he could hear a roaring sound that grew steadily louder.

"Perhaps this wasn't such a good idea!" he muttered.

As the boat swung round a corner he saw that he was heading for a waterfall. There was no escape! But at the last moment the boat

shook and ground to a halt on the very edge of the waterfall! He peeked over the side and saw that the water fell into a lake far below.

"Well I can't stay here, so I'd better jump," he thought bravely.

HE JUMPS!
TURN TO PAGE 38

29

Woollyfoot began to knot all the sheets together to make a rope. "I don't know if these will be enough. It's a very long way down," he muttered. He carefully began to pull one of the covers off the bed. Then it seemed to get stuck, so he pulled a bit harder.

"Oh dear!" he squeaked. He was staring straight into Cloudbanger's eyes. The giant had awakened!

"Thief!" roared Cloudbanger. Woollyfoot ran blindly toward the

window. The furious giant threw a pillow after him. It burst against the wall. Suddenly the air was filled with feathers.

"A-a-atiSHOO," sneezed the giant. Whoosh! Woollyfoot was blown right out of the window. As he spun through the air he could see a lake shimmering in the sunlight far below. Woollyfoot closed his eyes.

FALL INTO THE LAKE!
TURN TO PAGE
38

FALL INTO THE LAKE!
TURN TO PAGE
38

31

Woollyfoot began to climb down the path carefully. It was very steep, and most of the steps were cracked or broken. He kept slipping and sliding on the loose stones but slowly he could see that he was getting nearer and nearer to the bottom. But the farther down he went, the more difficult the path became.

Then when he was crawling gingerly along a very narrow part

of the path, he heard a loud rattling below him. It was Rumblewheel tearing past in a cloud of dust!

As Woollyfoot turned to look, he slipped again. There was nothing to hang on to. "Oh no!" he cried, as he slid helplessly down the mountain side. "Look out, Rumblewheel!"

HE FALLS! TURN TO PAGE 36

33

Woollyfoot chose the biggest sheet and knotted the corners together. He was dragging it to the window when he heard a loud yawn. Cloudbanger had woken up!

"Oh ho!" bellowed the giant when he saw Woollyfoot. "A little thief!" With a squeak of fright Woollyfoot leapt onto the windowsill, and gripping the corners of the sheet tightly, jumped high into the

air. The giant roared with anger as Woollyfoot floated away beneath his parachute.

"Phew!" gasped Woollyfoot. He looked to see where the parachute was taking him. He was flying across the lake toward a road. And there, to Woollyfoot's surprise, was Rumblewheel, pedaling furiously along.

"Oh dear," he cried. "I'm going to crash into him!" But if he let go, he would fall into the lake. What should he do?

LET GO 38

HANG ON 36

The last thing Woollyfoot saw before he landed with a thump was Rumblewheel's astonished face staring up at him. Then they both rolled over and over in a cloud of dust with the breath knocked right out of them!

"S-s-sorry, Rumblewheel," gasped Woollyfoot.

"Where on earth did you come from?" puffed the cyclist as he looked sadly at the battered cart beside him. "You've

broken my pedal. Now I'll never finish the race."

Woollyfoot felt ashamed. "It is only a race, Rumblewheel. I'll give you a push and help you get there."

The dusty cyclist began to laugh. "I've got an idea," he said. "Look! We're almost at the top of the hill that leads into the village. I can coast from there. Why don't we both finish together!"

GO TO THE HILLTOP! TURN TO PAGE 46

Splash! Woollyfoot landed in the water. He struggled to the nearest shore and started to wring out his wooly socks.

"Oh no," he thought as he looked about, "I'm on an island and it's too far to swim to the proper shore." Just then, a large, pink pelican waddled out of the water. It stared at the socks.

"My, oh, my!" it said. "What wonderful things. They would be

perfect for keeping my poor feet warm."

Woollyfoot didn't say anything. He was looking at a log by the water's edge. "Perhaps I could float across on that," he thought.

"Ah-hem," said the pelican, poking its beak at the socks. "Can I have these?"

HE GIVES HIS SOCKS 40

HE FLOATS AWAY 42

"Oh my, oh my!" chuckled the pelican as it put on the socks and pattered round and round. "What splendid feet I have now!" Woollyfoot was still looking glum. "What are you doing here anyway?" demanded the pelican.

"I was in a race," Woollyfoot replied sadly, "until I got stuck on this island."

"Stuck?" said the pelican. "You're not stuck. I'll carry you off!" The friendly bird scooped Woollyfoot into its huge beak and flapped

into the air. All the way across it chattered happily to itself, "My, oh, my, what wonderful things socks are, what warm feet I've got. My, oh, my!"

"Thank you," said Woollyfoot when they landed on the other side. And with a laugh and a wave he ran off toward Meadowfree—without his socks!

GO TO MEADOWFREE!
TURN TO PAGE
44

41

Woollyfoot lay on the log and pushed himself off from the bank. He started to paddle as hard as he could, but the wind kept blowing him back toward the island.

The pelican flapped slowly away and Woollyfoot thought, "If only I'd given him my socks, the pelican might have helped me."

Finally, when the wind dropped, Woollyfoot managed to reach the other shore, and ran as fast as he could toward Meadowfree. But too much time had been lost. As he raced over the last hill he saw Rumblewheel hurtle over the finishing line to the rousing cheers of the Glitterbrook villagers.

He thought of his selfishness with the pelican and said quietly, "Well, I suppose I didn't deserve to win. I'll know better next time." Then he smiled. "But I still think I'm the fastest."

THE END

Woollyfoot ran faster than he had ever run before and soon arrived at Meadowfree.

"I wonder where the finishing line actually is?" he panted as he raced onto the main street. There was no one in sight as he passed the first houses.

Then he turned a corner to see the whole village looking the other way. "Oh no!" he cried. "I'm at the wrong end!" He dashed madly toward the finishing line. The crowd gasped in amazement as Woollyfoot and Rumblewheel hurtled across the line at exactly the same time—but from different directions! How everybody laughed as they carried Woollyfoot and Rumblewheel shoulder high. Who could have guessed such an ending? And what a party they had!

THE END

Woollyfoot pushed the battered cart up the hill while Rumblewheel steered. From the top of the hill they could see the crowd far below. Which village would have a new champion?

"They're in for a surprise all right," chuckled Rumblewheel as Woollyfoot gave a push and jumped aboard. They sped down the steep hill and all the villagers peered into the cloud of dust to see who the winner was. There was a silence as the two skidded across the line and collapsed with laughter. Then everyone was laughing.

"I don't think," said Rumblewheel at the party afterward, "it really matters who won. Have another piece of cake!"

"Thank you, Rumblewheel," said Woollyfoot. "It was a great race —and a great finish!"

THE END